An ACORN STREET STORY

My tooth is WOBBLY!

This book belongs to

....

My tooth is wobbly!

A LAUGHING LOBSTER BOOK 978-1-914564-31-4

Published in Great Britain by Laughing Lobster, an imprint of Centum Publishing Ltd.
This edition published 2022.

1 3 5 7 9 10 8 6 4 2

Illustrations by Sue Mason.

Laughing Lobster, an imprint of Centum Publishing Ltd, 20 Devon Square, Newton Abbot, Devon, TQ12 2HR, UK. 9/10 Fenian St, Dublin 2, D02 RX24, Ireland.

books@centumpublishingltd.co.uk

LAUGHING LOBSTER, CENTUM PUBLISHING LIMITED Reg. No. 08497203

A CIP catalogue record for this book is available from the British Library.

Printed in China.

Meet the characters...

Hello, I'm **Noah!**

This is my **Mum** and my stepdad **Andy.**

This is **Grace,** my baby sister.

...And this is our house in **ACORN STREET!**

(My friends **Joe, Poppy** and **Mia** live on Acorn Street, too.)

My tooth is loose! I can wiggle it with my tongue.

Wibble wobble. Wibble wobble.

"That's good. It will fall out soon," says Mum.

I don't want my tooth to fall out.
It might hurt! I ask if we can keep
it in with sticky tape but Mum
shakes her head.

"Let me have a look, Noah. Open wide!" says Mum. I show her my loose tooth.

Wibble wobble.

"Don't worry. It's normal for a tooth to come out at your age and it won't hurt," she says. "These are your baby teeth but now new strong ones are growing underneath. They'll push out the baby teeth eventually."

"Do you mean that **all** my teeth are going to fall out?" I ask.
"Well, yes. But gradually, one by one. It'll be OK," says Mum.
This doesn't sound OK at all!

While Mum is at work, Grandma Lena comes round to take me
and Grace to the park.
"I can't go. My tooth is wobbling all over the place," I say as I
open my mouth to show her.

Wibble wobble.

"Keep moving it with your tongue. Before you know it . . . POP!"
she tells me. "Let's go and brush your teeth and then we can go."
I don't want it to POP out of my mouth. What if it happens when I'm
brushing my teeth and it hurts?

"Don't worry. We can make sure we brush your loose tooth gently," says Grandma Lena. "I'll teach you a song that will help you look after your new tooth too. Just copy me."

Squeeze the toothpaste.

Turn the tap.

Brush your teeth.

 *Clap, clap, clap!*

Grandma Lena's tooth song makes me feel a bit better. "I think I'll be all right to go to the park," I say, and she gives me a hug.

When we get to the park we see Poppy.
"Look!" I say as I open my mouth wide and wobble
my tooth with my tongue. It makes her laugh.

"Snap!" she says as she shows me her loose tooth too.
It wibble-wobbles even more than mine does!

"I can't wait until our teeth fall out," says Poppy. "Because I've got a storybook about pirates and they all have gaps in their teeth. We're going to look like pirates!"

Then we practise making pirate noises:

"Ahar! Ahoy!"

"I'll be Pirate Gaptooth!" I say.

"I'll be Pirate Notooth!" says Poppy.

"My big sister Hannah told me that if we put our baby teeth under our pillows at night time, the tooth fairy will visit us and leave us a surprise," says Poppy.

I'm so excited about the tooth fairy that I'm glad my tooth
is wobbly. I'm going to stay awake all night so I can see her.

The next morning my tooth is still hanging on, so I keep wiggling it with my tongue.

Wibble wobble. Wibble wobble.

"Try it again," says Mum, so I do . . . **Wibble wobble.**

Wibble wobble . . . until at last it comes out.
It doesn't POP though. It just slips out and it doesn't hurt at all.

When I hold it in my hand it looks tiny, like a white bead from Grandma Lena's necklace.

"Look in the mirror and smile," says Mum, so I do.
"Ahoy! I'm Pirate Gaptooth!" I tell Mum.
"I can see your new tooth peeping up already," says Mum. "You won't have your pirate gap for long."

That **exact** same day Poppy's wobbly tooth comes out. She shows me her gap when she comes round to play.
"It didn't hurt one bit!" she says.

"The tooth fairy is going to be busy tonight!" says Mum.

At bedtime, Mum gives me a piece of cotton wool to wrap up my baby tooth. I try to make the parcel really small, so it won't be too heavy for the tooth fairy. Then I hide it under my pillow.

I try really hard to stay awake but the next thing I know it's morning.

The tooth fairy must be the quietest, gentlest fairy ever, because I don't wake up at all when she visits. I know she came, though, because my tooth has gone.

In its place under the pillow, I find a gold coin.

It makes a clinking noise when I put it into my piggy bank.
Thank you, tooth fairy!

The next day Poppy is waiting at the park for me, along with Mia and Joe. I tell them all about my surprise from the tooth fairy.

"The tooth fairy left me some money, too," says Poppy.

"I can't wait for one of my teeth to go wobbly!" says Mia.

"And mine," says Joe.

"It doesn't hurt at all," I tell them and then I show them how to do Grandma Lena's tooth song.

Squeeze the toothpaste. Turn the tap.

Brush your teeth. Clap, clap, clap!

I hope the tooth fairy hasn't gone far. Because guess what?

Wibble wobble. Wibble wobble.

I've just got another wobbly tooth. Hooray!